TALES
OF THE
TRICKSTERS

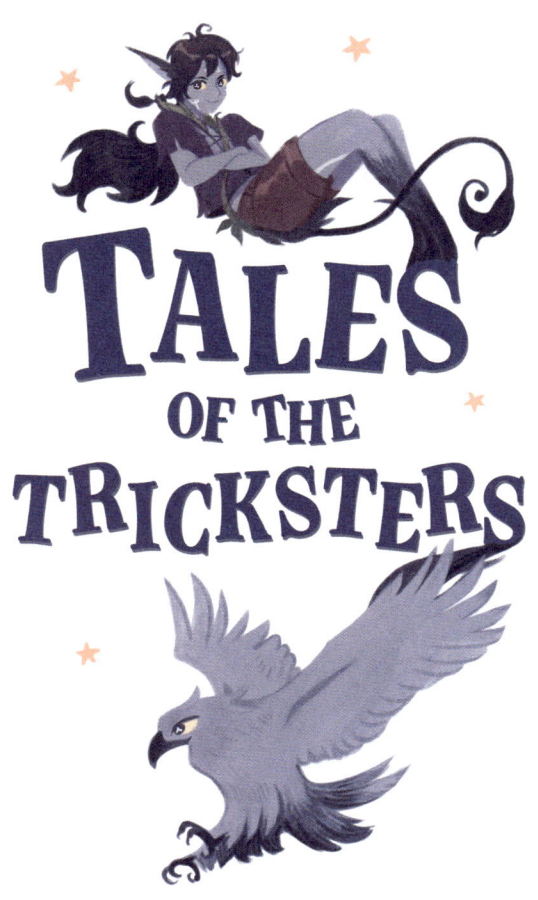

Tales of the Tricksters

Jonny Walker

Corinne Caro

Collins

CONTENTS

Chapter 1 What is a trickster? 2

The appearance of Pooka 14

Chapter 2 Hermes, the baby trickster. 16

More about Maia .26

Chapter 3 Delilah the Wily 28

One thousand and one nights. 40

Chapter 4 Anansi and Aso 42

Tricksters love food. 52

Chapter 5 Kitsune, trickster fox. 54

Rambo, the real fox trickster 66

Chapter 6 Pooka, the best trickster 68

Who were the banshees? 80

Map of the tricksters. 82

How do we know these old stories? 84

About the author 86

About the illustrator. 88

Book chat. 90

CHAPTER 1
WHAT IS A TRICKSTER?

You're new here, I think? I'll be your guide – you can trust me. I promise!

The people in the village call me all sorts of things. Some call me a scamp, some call me a creature. Some even say I can never be trusted.

Personally, I think I'm cute.

And trustworthy! Definitely trustworthy.

My name is Pooka, by the way. I'm pleased to meet you.

Anyway, come and sit with me. I'm going to tell you all about tricksters, and what makes us – pardon my mistake – what makes *them* so special.

Across the world, people tell tales of tricksters.

Tricksters are mysterious individuals who bend and break the rules. Some have the power to get their own way through trickery. Some can transform their appearance. Some can make you think differently. Some can solve problems in unusual ways.

Tricksters may help you or they may harm you. They can make you laugh one minute, and make you cry the next.

Some of them look cute sitting on a rock, or so I'm told.

Many tricksters are shapeshifters, which means they can change their appearance to look like other creatures.

In Viking myths, the Norse trickster god Loki once turned himself into a mare, to distract a stallion! What a cool thing to do!

Pooka fact

In Irish folklore, Pooka was said to take the form of a sleek-coated wild horse. They would gallop through the fields, destroying crops and smashing fences in an act of playful mischief.

Ignore that. That is gossip, and gossipers are liars.

In the Yoruba myths of West Africa, Eshu is the trickster orisha. Orisha means "godly being".

Most orishas rule in one place only. Eshu doesn't live only in the seas, or only in the fires or the skies. He wants to go wherever he chooses!

He's a messenger and a traveller – a bit like Hermes, and I'll tell you more about *him* in a minute. Some say Eshu is old, and some say he's young. He's a super-shapeshifter. He's all things to all people.

Most tricksters have an enormous appetite. Lots of trickster tales are about the battle against hunger and the endless search for delicious food.

What's your favourite food? Think of it now. I'm thinking of mine. Oh great, and now I'm salivating!

Tricksters never forget the most important thing – they always want a full stomach.

Tricksters can be motivated by lots of different emotions. For example, they might want revenge, they might want to spread chaos or they might just want to make themselves laugh.

Tanuki are tricksters in Japanese folktales. Tanuki have a pot belly, which is meant to show their calm, relaxed approach to life. Tanuki use their belly like a drum, bashing a rhythm on it.

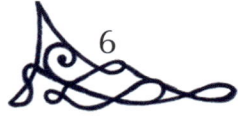

They are excellent shapeshifters, and they can impersonate animals and humans. Their favourite shape to shift into is ... don't laugh ... a tea kettle!

This transformation originally happened when a Tanuki wanted to make itself into something useful, as a thank-you present for a human. The Tanuki had a surprise when the kettle was heated!

Tricksters work in sneaky ways to get what they want. These experts of deception can be very intelligent and very cheeky, and often both at the same time!

It's very easy to underestimate the mind of a trickster, especially when they're so good at entertaining us with their ... peculiar behaviours.

There's always a reason why they do what they do, even if you don't understand it. Tricksters always seem to create their own odd logic.

One particular Greek goddess always used to entertain herself in mischievous ways.

Atë (say: *ah-tay*) was the Greek goddess of trickery.

She tricked a satyr – half-goat, half human – into trying to ride on a wild bull's back. She did this by telling the satyr that it would impress Dionysus, the god of parties and celebration.

The satyr fell off, of course, and Atë simply laughed and ran away.

Tricksters are unpredictable – you never know what they will do next. Tricksters can do very kind and brave things, but they might also play a cruel prank on you. They might do good deeds in bad ways, and bad deeds in good ways.

This towering trickster from Belgium is called Lange Wapper, which translates as Long Flapper. He played terrifying pranks on people in the city of Antwerp. But usually, he would choose to trick those who were mistreating other people. He would shapeshift to a giant size and scare them so much, they would leave the city.

OK, let me see what we've got so far.

- Tricksters like to shapeshift.
- Tricksters always do things for a reason (even if it's not obvious).
- Tricksters love food and they're always hungry.

So that's my introduction to tricksters, new friend. You'll find them in old stories from all over the world. Wherever there are rules, there are tricksters sneakily breaking them, in unusual ways.

I've got some excellent trickster tales that I can tell you, if you are not too busy?

Here, let me give you a ride into the village. Go on. Hop up on.

Yep. It's still me, but I'm a horse now. Come on!

THE APPEARANCE OF POOKA

BEFORE

thinking of devious and unusual plans

cheeky grin

doing whatever it takes to satisfy the hunger

AFTER

still thinking of
devious plans

legs to go wherever
it wants to go

15

CHAPTER 2
HERMES, THE BABY TRICKSTER

Hey, look over there! It's a postal worker, dropping off letters and parcels. You know … this makes me think of Hermes.

Have you heard of him? Hermes was the messenger god in ancient Greek myths. His mother was Maia, a peaceful mountain goddess who lived alone in a cave. His father was Zeus, King of the Gods.

Hermes loved chatting to anyone who would listen. Tricksters love having unexpected conversations.

Hermes was a trickster from the moment he was born ...

Pooka fact

You can find the messenger god in both Roman and Greek myths. The Romans called him Mercury.

Maia loved the calm within her cave, but it disappeared moments after she gave birth to Hermes. Before he learnt to cry, Hermes learnt to speak.

"Hiya! What a spectacular joy it is to be alive! Thanks for creating me, mother. That was generous. I'm off exploring; see you in a bit!" the baby said, pointing to the entrance of the cave.

Maia smiled in amusement at her instantly chatty infant. As one of the timeless goddesses of the mountains, nothing really surprised her anymore.

"OK, sweet child, let me rest. Enjoy exploring our world!" she said with a smile.

Hermes crawled out from the cave and looked around him. He smiled at the golden light that shimmered over the dancing blades of grass. He giggled at the seedheads that floated away from the swaying dandelions.

"Nature is joyful," he squealed. Then his eyes widened. "What ... on Earth ... are they?!"

The awestruck Hermes had spotted a tortoise, an ox and a sheep.

He ran towards the three animals, with open arms.

Pooka fact
Sprinting babies are terrifying.

Hermes had a curious mind. Looking at the three creatures, he began scratching his head. An idea was forming.

I wonder ... he thought, *if I could combine them?*

The animals had given Hermes an amazing idea for a new musical instrument called a lyre. But you can't play an *imaginary* instrument.

He flexed his muscles, preparing himself for action.

"Come here, creatures!" he shouted, chasing and catching each one of them, giggling as he did so.

At this point in the story, I want to interrupt, because I'm a very helpful Pooka.

So that I don't have to describe the yucky bits, I'll just say this. The tortoise "became an empty shell". The ox "became a very useful pair of horns". And the sheep's intestines "were pulled tight like string".

OK, now that we know what happened there, let's see what he did with them.

Hermes raised the ox horns high above his head and smashed them down hard into the tortoise shell. Around the horns, he wove the sheep "string" and pulled it tight. He wrapped it around until there were seven strings.

"Ta-da!" he shouted and began plucking the strings. Each one made a different musical note. His invention worked!

Pooka fact

Sheep guts really were used to make lyre strings.

Hermes played the first song on the lyre and sang along to it happily. But then he saw something else …

"Glorious! COWS! I want them," he shouted, pointing to a field of cattle. "They can be my playmates!"

Little did Hermes know that the cows belonged to his half-brother, Apollo. Apollo was the mighty god of light.

"How could I steal these cows without leaving any evidence?" the young trickster asked himself.

"Aha!" He had a plan. "For this to work, I'll need many shoes."

And so he ran into the village, stole 24 pairs of shoes for the 12 cows, and hurried back to the field.

He giggled to himself at the brilliance of his plan. He put one shoe onto each hoof of each cow. But he put the shoes on backwards.

This meant that when the cows walked in one direction, the tracks they created made it look like they had gone the opposite way!

And instead of hoof-tracks, the cows left tracks that resembled human footprints.

"The perfect trick!" Hermes chuckled. He led the 12 cows out of the field, back home to Maia.

As he entered, Maia stirred from her sleep.

"How was your first experience of the world?" she asked, rubbing her eyes.

"Splendid, Mother! I had a perfectly mischief-free day."

She peered suspiciously at the tortoise-and-ox instrument, which Hermes tried to hide behind his back.

Suddenly, Apollo, god of the Sun, burst into the cave in a dazzling blast of brightness! "That pesky little thief! Maia, that baby stole my special cows! I followed their prints and they led me to nowhere. So I followed them backwards ... and they're all mooing outside your cave!"

"Sorry, brother!" Hermes said, patting Apollo on the leg.

"Whoah! It speaks already!" Apollo yelped.

"Indeed I do, brother, please don't be angry with me. I've made something for you ... look!"

Hermes handed the tortoise-lyre to Apollo.

"Sing, Apollo," Hermes said. "Go on!"

And Apollo did sing, and he strummed the lyre, and the most beautiful music filled the cave, the sweetest sounds there had ever been. Maia danced with her mysterious child.

In that moment, Apollo became the god of music. And it would not have happened without Hermes, the tiny talking trickster.

MORE ABOUT MAIA

In mythology, Maia is one of seven sisters, who are known as the "Pleiades" (say: *play-a-deez*).

Maia was known as "Mountain Maia with the lively eyes", and she was the wise eldest sister.

The Pleiades is also the name of a cluster of stars, also known as the Seven Sisters. The Greeks used these stars to help them navigate across the seas.

For the Maōri people of Aotearoa New Zealand, the new year begins when these stars are first seen in the sky. The Maōri name for the Pleiades star cluster is Matariki.

CHAPTER 3
DELILAH THE WILY

Wow! Look at the size of that mansion on the hill!

I'd enjoy having all of those rooms to race around in.

You know … this reminds me of a story told over a thousand years ago, about somebody else who wished to live in the grandest house in the neighbourhood.

Let me tell you about Delilah.

Harun al-Rashid, the ruler of Baghdad, needed to recruit two new captains to help manage the city. Captains are powerful and well-paid. He needed to find two well-respected and trustworthy people.

Unfortunately, Harun al-Rashid found Calamity Ahmed and Hasan the Pest. Everybody in the city knew these two men were only good at deceiving people into giving them money. However, stories of their trickery had not reached Harun al-Rashid's palace.

Pooka fact

Baghdad is a very old city in the country of Iraq.

When the two crooks arrived at the palace, lying about their achievements, Harun al-Rashid invited them to become captains.

This angered Delilah, who lived with her daughter Zainab. Years before, her husband served Harun al-Rashid as Chief Messenger. After he died, Delilah and Zainab were forced to leave the palace and move into a small mud brick house.

"You know what I'm sick of, Zainab?" Delilah asked, chewing a mouthful of pistachios. "Fools like Calamity Ahmed and Hasan the Pest tricking their way to the top! If *anybody* should have deceived their way to power, it's me!"

She chucked the pistachio shells out of the window.

"What's the plan, Mother?" Zainab asked.

"I'll show Harun al-Rashid how clever I am – " Delilah replied.

Delilah imagined that if she could demonstrate her intelligence through stunning acts of trickery, perhaps Harun al-Rashid would reward her too. She and Zainab could live in luxury again.

First, Delilah visited the shoemaker. She fell to her knees, weeping. "Oh, shoemaker! My wealthy husband is in a horrible situation!"

"What situation?" asked the shoemaker.

"His shoes were stolen! Today he must meet an important trader from Cairo. He will feel embarrassed to be shoeless!"

The shoemaker frowned.

"Unfortunately," she continued, "I have no coins with me. If you give me your finest pair now, my husband will pay you *triple* the price tomorrow."

This deal pleased the shoemaker. He nodded, and Delilah grabbed the most expensive pair of leather shoes.

"Many blessings, shoemaker!" she shouted, tossing the shoes into her sack.

Delilah spent the entire day sneaking around in this way, tricking traders with made-up stories and filling her sack with expensive goods. After 15 tricks, the sack was too heavy to carry.

Across Baghdad's marketplaces, there were shouts of: "That sneaky woman must have tricked me!" and "Punish her!"

Delilah wrapped her shawl tightly around her, hiding her identity and her laughter.

A teenager passed by with his donkey.

"Come here!" called Delilah. "It's your lucky day, donkey-boy!"

"Is it?" he replied.

"Yes! I'm from a wealthy family. I've been praying to find a husband for my daughter. In a dream, I saw her with a handsome young man, riding a donkey into our enormous palace."

"Okaaaay ..." he said.

"It was you in my dream! It's a sign! You will live a life of luxury with us!"

The boy scratched his head in disbelief.

Delilah continued. "Give me your donkey! I'll rush home to tell Zainab the news!"

The boy believed Delilah, and handed her the donkey's reins.

"I'll wait here?" he asked.

"Whatever!" Delilah said, clambering atop the donkey with her sackful of loot.

Delilah arrived home to find Zainab and an angry mob waiting for her. Zainab grinned at her naughty mother.

"That's her!" roared the shoemaker.

"Return my scissors!" shouted the barber.

"Gold thief!!" wept the jeweller.

The enraged crowd had attracted the attention of the stony-faced police captain too.

"Stop yapping, you lot!" Delilah shouted. "You'll get your stuff back. I have my reasons – "

The police captain grabbed her. "Enough words! I'm taking you to jail."

"Or," Delilah said, shaking her head, "if you want to know about all the *other* things I've stolen, take me to Harun al-Rashid instead. I will confess everything to him. You'll be rewarded for stopping me, Sir!"

This idea pleased the police captain. The market traders took their possessions from the sack, and Delilah asked Zainab to return the boy's donkey.

At the palace, Delilah knelt before Harun al-Rashid.

The ruler said, "So you're the woman who has spread chaos in my city today."

"Yep," Delilah said, nibbling her thumbnail casually. "I have my reasons – "

Delilah told the ruler about her day of mischief, lies and disguises – how she tricked the shoemaker, the donkey-boy, and everyone else ...

She explained that she'd only been trying to prove her cleverness to him. "You could use somebody with my skill set, right? You employed my husband before. Perhaps you could employ me and my daughter Zainab. You could use our abilities for good, not for mischief."

Harun al-Rashid shook his head in amused disbelief at the fearless woman. They laughed together.

"You hired those fools Calamity Ahmed and Hasan the Pest ... hire me too!"

"OK ... Delilah the Wily!" the ruler joked. This nickname stuck, and she's still called this today.

Harun al-Rashid made Delilah his most important chief adviser, and young Zainab became the next chief messenger of the city.

ONE THOUSAND AND ONE NIGHTS

The story of Delilah the Wily is very old. It is one of the many stories featured in *One Thousand and One Nights*, which is also known as "Arabian Nights".

The stories are a collection of tales that were told and retold over a thousand years ago, across Asia, North Africa and the Middle East.

These amazing stories vary enormously in style. We have trickster tales, like that of Delilah, but there are also stories of space travel, pirates and even robots!

The most well-known story today is probably "Aladdin", which introduced readers to magic carpets and genies trapped in lamps.

CHAPTER 4
ANANSI AND ASO

What's all that shouting?!

Oh look, that man is terrified of a tiny spider!

Some of the most famous tricksters in the world were spiders ... such as the cunning husband and wife duo, Anansi and Aso.

Stories of Anansi and Aso began in West Africa. They are still told there, as well as in North America and the Caribbean.

These tricksters might not be big, but they still find a way to stand up for themselves.

Anansi is known by different names – Ananse, Aunt Nancy, Kwaku Ananse – but is often shown as spider-like.

Anansi loves food. Many of his stories involve getting food by trickery. Anansi uses his cunning to get what he wants from lots of different characters, mostly animals.

Listen up ... I'm inspired by this panic. Let me tell you some spider stories.

WHY IS JANKRO BALD?

Whenever Anansi or Aso tried to cook, Jankro the turkey vulture flew down and stole their vegetables.

Aso invented a trick to teach the vulture a lesson.

She found Jankro at the market and tapped his head. "Anansi and I are getting married, Jankro! Please be a guest at our wedding." Jankro was surprised but agreed.

Jankro arrived at Anansi and Aso's house, and noticed he was the only guest.

"Is it just us?" Jankro asked, his beady bird-eyes darting between Aso, Anansi and the table full of food.

"The food will keep us company," replied Anansi.

They guzzled baked yams, then washed them down with fruit juice.

This is when Anansi's plan kicked into action.

"The next part of the ceremony involves water. I've got the water ready to put on our heads," Anansi said. "You first, Jankro."

Jankro waddled over to the copper pot. He did not know that the water was boiling hot.

"Pop your head in there," Anansi said.

Jankro did, and it was so hot, his feathers fell out.

And that's why Jankro has a bald head today.

Pooka fact

Jankro, or John Crow, is the name given to the turkey vulture in Jamaica.

ASO TRICKS THE TIGER

Tiger was hungry. She knew everybody feared her, so she decided to intimidate her neighbours into giving her some food.

There was a knock on Aso and Anansi's door. It was Tiger.

"Feed me," said Tiger.

"Sorry, Tiger. We have no food at all," Aso said, faking a sad voice.

Anansi, who hadn't heard the knocking, shouted, "Come, children! Dinner's ready!"

"You're lying, Aso! FEED ME!" roared Tiger.

"OK, fine," Aso said, "but you must follow my instructions exactly."

Aso climbed into the cooking pot. "Look, Tiger. When I knock on the lid, you must let me out, OK?" Aso said.

So Tiger put the lid on the pot, and a few moments later, Aso banged on the lid, and Tiger let her climb out.

"Wonderful!" said Aso. "That was perfect! Next, it's your turn. Climb inside, Tiger."

Tiger climbed in, and Aso and Anasi slammed the lid down. Tiger banged her claws on it, but the two spiders did not let Tiger out.

"Dinnertime!" Anansi shouted.

Tiger did not go home that night, and Anansi and Aso went to bed with full stomachs.

THE BEAN THIEF

Aso and Anansi were putting on their finest garments. They were visiting Aso's parents for a party and wanted to make a good impression.

So Anansi balanced his smart top hat on his head. When they arrived at the party, everybody turned to look at them.

"It's me ... Fancy Anansi!" Anansi boasted, tapping his hat.

Aso enjoyed sharing stories with her family, whilst Anansi guarded the food table.

Anansi had a full plate in each hand, and whilst his mouth was chewing, his eyes were searching.

"Where are those delicious beans?" he wondered.

Aso's parents made the tastiest beans in the land. Anansi suspected Aso's father had hidden them for himself – he loved them too.

Anansi scuttled over to Aso's father, trickery brewing in his mind. "Pardon me, Sir. May I go to the kitchen to thank the chef?" Anansi asked.

"Of course! What lovely manners," Aso's father replied.

Anansi had other plans, of course.

In the kitchen, he spotted something bubbling away on the stove.

"*My* beans!" Anansi whispered, overjoyed. "I'll be taking *these*."

Anansi began scooping hot, spicy beans into a bag.

Then he tied up the bag (though spiders are poor at tying knots), and placed it on his head. He rested his top hat over it.

"I'll enjoy chomping these back at home!" he chuckled.

He went to look for Aso. He wanted to get home quickly, as the beans were hot. But Aso's mother was making a speech.

"Here he is! Let's celebrate Anansi, who makes our daughter so happy! Let's sing for Anansi!"

The guests began singing, whilst the top of Anansi's head got hotter and hotter.

"Is this a long song?" Anansi asked, sweating. Everyone ignored him and carried on singing.

It was unbearable. He lifted his hat, and scorching beans poured out all over him. The singing stopped abruptly.

Aso grabbed Anansi over her shoulder and dashed out of the front door.

"Sharing is caring!" she laughed, as she plucked a hot bean off his head and ate it.

TRICKSTERS LOVE FOOD

When you explore lots of different trickster tales, you'll notice that lots of them are about eating and drinking.

In Greek mythology, Tantalus tricked the gods, so they punished him with a trick of their own. He was sent to sit in a pool of water, with delicious fruits above him. But when he tried to drink, the water always dropped away from him. And when he tried to eat, the fruits slipped further out of reach.

This is where we get the word "tantalising", which means to tease somebody by offering them something they can't have.

CHAPTER 5
KITSUNE, TRICKSTER FOX

Hey, look over there! A family of foxes – a dog, a vixen and their little cub – sprinting across the field.

I think foxes have a mysterious beauty, in the way they burst out in a flash of red, like a darting flame.

Funnily enough, foxes are seen as nature's tricksters.

Around the world, there are many trickster tales about cunning and sly foxes.

But the country with the most famous fox tricksters is Japan.

Kitsune are shapeshifting foxes. They grow additional tails every hundred years, and the ten-tailed kitsune turn white, on their thousandth birthday!

Kitsune are mischievous in some stories, but the tale I want to tell is different.

The kitsune are tricksters because they can shapeshift, but instead of using this power only for mischief and trickery, they can also use it to support humans.

Grab a tissue; *this* trickster tale is heartbreaking!

Pooka fact

Baby foxes are called "kits" or "pups".

KUZONOHA, THE KITSUNE

Over one thousand years ago, there lived a poor man who was facing an enormous challenge.

Abe no Yasuna grew up in a very wealthy family, but that all changed one fateful day, when his father was visited by a smooth-talking stranger. The stranger persuaded his father to trust him, but then he escaped with all of the family's money.

When Abe no Yasuna grew to be an adult, his life was still a struggle. His rickety house was damaged, and he was working hard to repair it.

As often as he could, he visited a shrine in the Shinoda Forest, to give blessings in the hope of receiving good fortune.

One day, as he walked through the forest, he was startled by a flash of snowy fur darting towards him. It was a white fox, with an enormous fountain of tails trailing behind it.

"Stranger, help me! A hunter is chasing me. I need you to cover my tracks so I can escape. Where should I run?" the fox asked him.

Quick-thinking Abe no Yasuna directed the fox to race down one particular path.

"Go this way, fox. It leads to the densest part of the forest – you can hide there."

The fox escaped, then the hunter arrived.

"Oy!" the hunter shouted. "Where did the fox go? It must have run straight past you!"

"I'm sorry, I'd help you if I could, but I didn't see a fox."

The foul-tempered hunter barged past him, knocking Abe no Yasuna to the ground.

A woman emerged from between the trees and ran over to help. "That must have hurt!" she said. "Let me help you … my name is Kuzonoha."

Kuzonoha pulled Abe no Yasuna to his feet. They walked together through the Shinoda Forest.

"So … what were *you* doing out here?" he asked.

"I was just … exercising," she smiled.

They both decided they would enjoy walking together more often. As the weeks went by, they fell in love. When the time felt right, they got married. Their wedding took place on a bright and rainy day, and the sky seemed to light up with mysterious torches.

Pooka fact

Sometimes the sun shines while it's raining. In Japan, this is called a "fox wedding", based on kitsune myths.

Soon after that, they had a son. For several years, they enjoyed a peaceful, regular life at home. They didn't have much money, but they had love, they had laughter and they had each other.

Around five years passed, and Kuzonoha was telling a bedtime story to her young son. The boy smiled up at his mother as she told him fantastic tales of the animals of the forest.

But then, in the flicker of the candlelight, he noticed something strange. His mother's shadow on the wall looked wrong. It was a fox's shadow.

Kuzonoha followed his gaze and saw what he was looking at. She blew out the candle.

"That's enough story, child." She kissed his head and ran out of the room, her heart racing.

Kitsune can only remain living among humans if their true identity remains unknown.

The child knew what he had seen, and Kuzonoha knew that he had seen it.

Her secret was revealed. She *was* the white fox that Abe no Yasuna had saved, all those years ago.

Kuzonoha had no choice but to leave the family she loved behind.

This was the sad fact of life as a kitsune.

She wrote a note and left it for Abe no Yasuna.

Speak to our son. If you still love me, find me in the forest where you met me.

After reading the note, Abe no Yasuna was confused, so he called his son over to speak to him.

The boy told his father about the strange event the night before. "Dad, when I saw Mum's shadow, it was … fox-shaped."

His father thought back to the day he met Kuzonoha. He remembered the fox he encountered just seconds before.

Then he knew the sad truth too.

Abe no Yasuna and the boy loved Kuzonoha, whether she was a fox, a human, or anything in between.

So they raced together to the Shinoda Forest, to see her one last time.

She embraced them, told them she loved them, and then returned to her fox form.

RAMBO, THE REAL FOX TRICKSTER

In New South Wales, in Australia, conservationists wanted to create a safe area in the forests, so that they could reintroduce some endangered mammals, like the bilby. But to do that, they had to make sure there were no other predators in the safe area.

A red fox – named Rambo by those who tried to catch him – refused to be removed!

Rambo managed to avoid capture for over four years. He dodged over 10,000 traps, and over 50 days of being chased by hunting dogs.

And like a true trickster, he teased the hunters by appearing on their cameras, before disappearing.

a bilby

CHAPTER 6
POOKA, THE BEST TRICKSTER

Let me tell you about one more trickster.

They're a shapeshifter who loves the countryside. They enjoy chatting. They can appear as a trustworthy horse that loves to take people on adventures …

It's me! I'm biased, but I think I am the best trickster.

I'm well known in Ireland, and lots of other places too.

In the olden days, stories were shared about me and my mischief in Cornwall, Wales, Norway, Iceland, Denmark, and even as far away as Latvia!

Some people say I'm a goblin. In some tales, I'm a horse.

In Latvia, they say I'm a fiery ball who loves milk!

Some say I have an odd relationship with blackberries.

You're safe picking blackberries until October. But from the first of November, you should never pick them!

She's right. I heard that on the night before November, Pooka sneezes all over the berries and covers them in Pooka slime.

The most famous story about me involves my favourite prank – let's call it ... social sprinting.

There's nothing I enjoy more than dashing through the countryside, and it's much more fun with a friend. I find people who are wandering about, pick them up and give them an unexpected high-speed shoulder-ride!

And if I can teach them a life lesson along the way ... even better!

I do not leave slime on berries.

POOKA AND THE PIPER

A widow and her son lived in a ramshackle old cottage.

The boy often got into trouble. He was impulsive and did things without thinking. If he saw something he wanted, sometimes he would take it. He preferred bending the truth rather than telling it.

The boy had one dream in life – to be a piper. He practised his performances daily, but no matter how hard he tried, he could remember only one song.

The boy travelled around the village, performing his song for people who would give him a few coins.

Once, this impulsive boy stole a goose from the neighbour's farm. He pretended it was his own, and sold it at the market!

His mother was disappointed when she found out. She told him to go for a long hike to the Reek (a huge mountain) to think about his actions.

The boy set off walking, and that's when playful Pooka spotted him.

Pooka, towering tall on two sturdy legs, sprinted up behind him, and flung the piper up onto their shoulders. Pooka carried the boy into the night.

"Hey! Put me down, pesky Pooka! I've no time for your games! I'm meant to be reflecting on my poor life choices!" the boy shouted.

Laughing, Pooka carried on running, and said, "Play me a song, piper!"

The boy started playing his tune.

"A different song!" shouted Pooka.

"I don't know any others!"

"Just play ... I'll put the tune in your head."

Without any mistakes, the piper played a tune he'd never learnt!

"Told you!" said Pooka. "You can share your new song when we get to the Hall of the Banshees, at the top of the Reek."

"The Reek! Oh, that's handy," the piper said. "My mother sent me there to reflect on my goose theft."

Pooka carried the boy over bogs and hills until they arrived at the huge wooden door of the Hall of the Banshees.

Pooka bashed on the door, and it opened onto a group of women of all ages sitting at a vast table covered with sumptuous food.

"Ah, welcome, Pooka. Who's this kid?"

"This," Pooka said, "is the best piper in all of Ireland!"

Then something even more unexpected happened.

A gigantic goose waddled out and began serving food to the banshees!

"That marking on the goose's head! That's the goose I stole! It's enormous ... how is this happening?" said the boy.

Pooka interrupted him. "Some things don't make sense, boy. Just play the pipe!"

The women danced to the perfect melodies of the piper. At the end of the evening, the banshees gave him a gold coin, and the goose gave him a new set of pipes.

The boy left his old pipes in the Hall of the Banshees.

"Let me get you home now," said Pooka.

When he returned home, the excited boy told his mother about his evening performing songs for the banshees.

She laughed, not believing him, as she was used to his tall tales.

"Listen!" he said, grabbing his new pipes and placing the coin on the table. He played, but the noise was hideous. It sounded as if all the world's geese were screeching at once!

"Practice makes perfect!" his mother shouted.

He lowered his pipes as he realised something. "You know what?" he said. "I think Pooka took me to the Reek to teach me a lesson about stealing the goose. Actions have consequences."

His mother patted his shoulder kindly, still not believing his story. She frowned at the table. "Where did that come from?"

Where the gold coin had been, there was now a single green leaf.

That was my story. I'm quite the trickster, aren't I?

Look around. It's just like I promised – we're back where we began.

Thanks for coming along for the ride.

We tricksters are an interesting bunch, don't you agree?

Imagine how boring life would be without us!

BONUS

WHO WERE THE BANSHEES?

Banshees were supernatural figures in old Irish stories, who were famed for their screams and cries. The banshees' screams were a sign that bad fortune was on the way.

Banshees are seen as being very mysterious. They do not have their own names, and their appearance can vary enormously. Banshees come in all ages, shapes and sizes.

In Irish folktales, banshees were not seen to be enemies or monsters. They were seen as simply another aspect of the world we share with fairies.

BONUS

MAP OF THE TRICKSTERS

The myths and folktales in this book come from around the world.

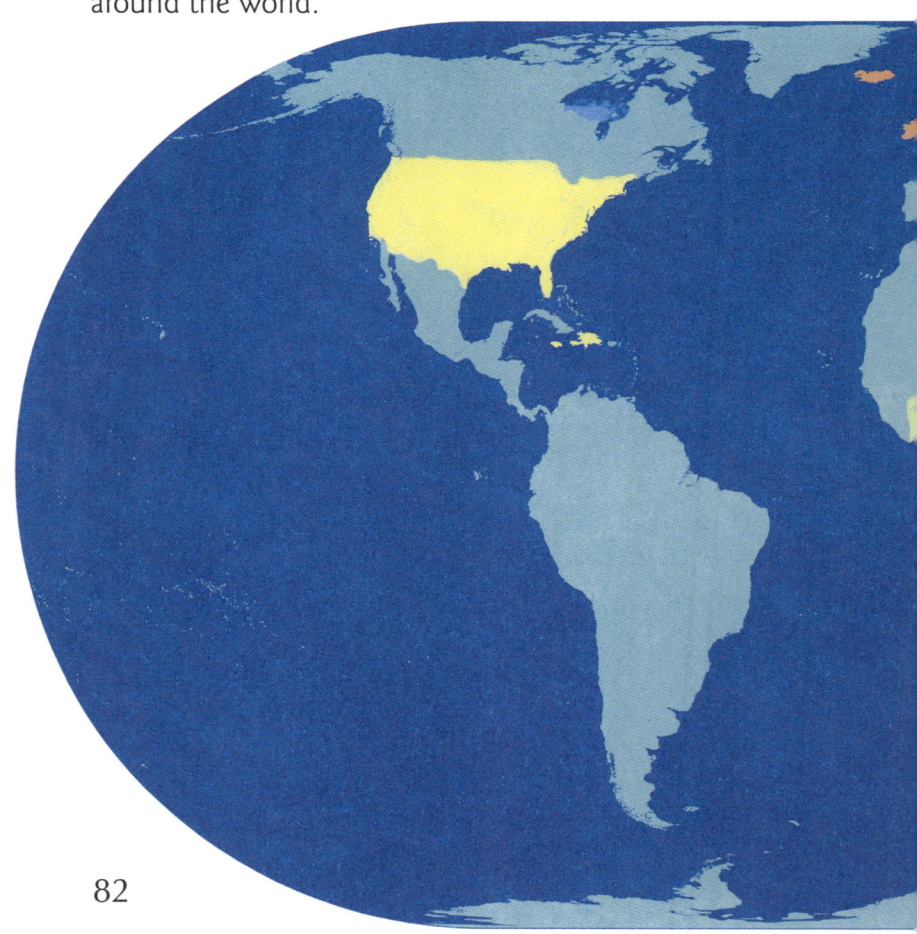

- Pooka
- Hermes
- Delilah the Wily
- Kitsune
- Ananasi and Aso

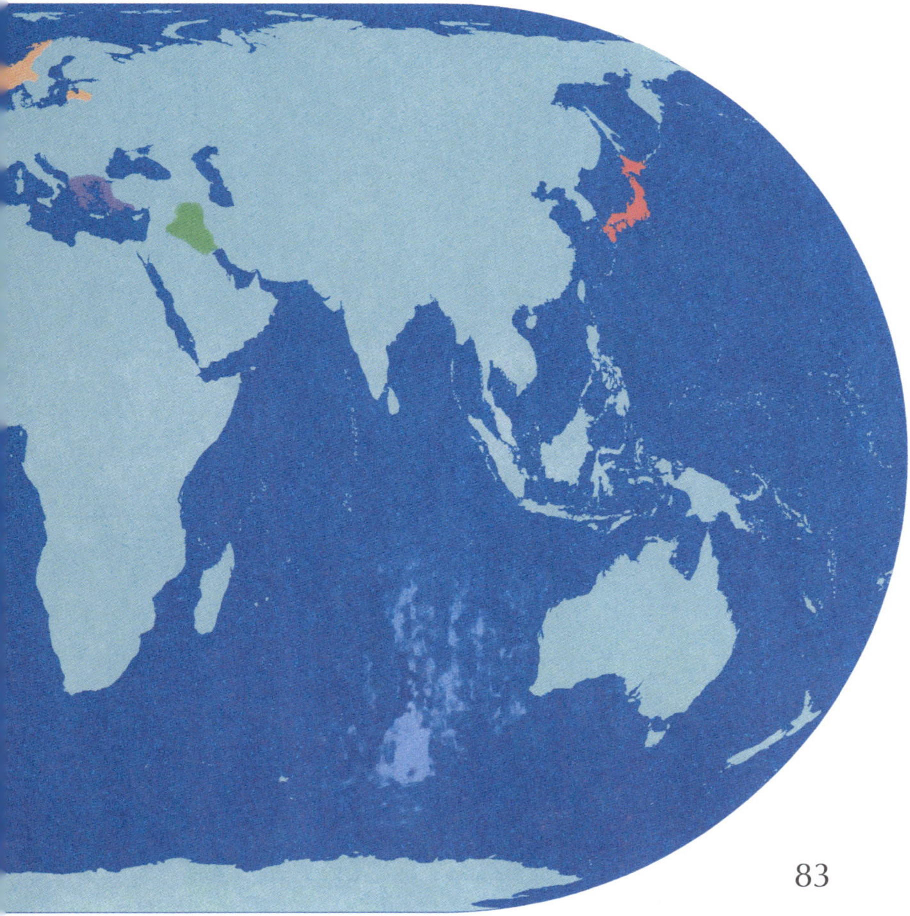

BONUS

HOW DO WE KNOW THESE OLD STORIES?

WORD OF MOUTH

Tales like the Anansi stories are often passed along when somebody shares them in conversation. Older family members may tell the stories to their young relatives.

POETRY

Many Greek myths – like the tale of Hermes – are known today because poets wrote them down in ancient texts.

STORY COLLECTORS

Lots of folktales are well-known today because they were written down into collections. *One Thousand and One Nights*, which includes Delilah the Wily, was a collection of stories gathered from across Asia and North Africa.

About the author

Why did you want to become a writer?
I've got a lot of ideas buzzing around in my head, and writing is a good way to tame them.

What non-fiction books did you like when you were young?
I was obsessed with "Strange But True", books about unsolved mysteries.

Jonny Walker

Why did you choose to write about trickster tales from different cultures?
I started off by developing expertise in Greek mythology, and my mythology students wanted me to teach them about other places too.

How did you decide which trickster stories to include in your book?
It was tricky! I chose the tricksters whose stories would be interesting, and I looked for the stories that were both funny and complex.

What was the hardest part of writing *Tales of the Tricksters*?
The research was hard, because lots of these stories were shared by word-of-mouth, not written down. There is very little written about Pooka. I even translated some Irish children's notebooks from a hundred years ago to find some Pooka tales!

What interests you about trickster characters?
Tricksters bend the rules and make you think. They're not the heroes, but they're not the villains either. They work in mysterious ways, which makes them fascinating characters.

How do trickster tales help us learn about different cultures?
Their similarities are a reminder of what we all have in common. No matter where we are in the world, people experience similar deep feelings about life, death, love, survival and happiness.

What's the best part about sharing myths and stories with readers?
I am a bit like that pesky Pooka because what I love most is chatting about life. I love sharing the stories, but I'm even more interested in what they make readers think about. You might think totally differently to anybody else, and that's great.

If you could be any trickster from the book, who would you be and why?
I am tempted to be the milk-drinking fireball version of Pooka, just to confuse my family.

What advice do you have for people who want to learn about mythology?
Read read read. The more myths you learn, the more they'll whisper their secret life lessons to you. You'll start spotting mythical links everywhere you go.

About the illustrator

Did you always want to be an illustrator?

Yes! I got into drawing during my high school days and aimed to become an illustrator after that.

How did you get into illustration?

It took me a while to figure out that I loved drawing stories as well as places. Once that sunk in, I knew that it would be my main passion!

Corinne Caro

What do you use to illustrate?

I use drawing programs on my computer. In my free time, I'm trying to learn traditional ways of painting as well, such as watercolor and gouache.

What was the best thing about illustrating this book?

The best thing was being able to read so many fun stories and learning more about other cultures. I hope I was able to convey the energy the stories had through my drawings!

Which myth did you like best and why?

My favourite would be the Kitsune myth as I love bittersweet stories! I had lots of fun illustrating those scenes.

How did you decide what the Pooka should look like?
I wanted to depict them as someone living a carefree life. So I gave them comfortable clothes that let them move as much as they can. I also imagine them having long unruly hair which helps depict their mischief.

If you could be any trickster from the book which would you want to be?
I'd definitely want to be like Pooka! They're such a free spirited one, and I like the idea of transforming into different animals and going wherever they like to.

Did you learn anything while illustrating this book?
It was really fun to look up each culture and find references for each trickster. They all had such unique looks but it was cool to see that they had similar energy and stories.

What was the most difficult thing?
Anansi and Aso were a bit difficult to draw. I wanted them to look spider-y in their human forms, without being too unapproachable. I really love how mischievous their stories were so I really enjoyed illustrating their parts!

Which scene was the most fun to draw?
I really had fun drawing the spread with all the tricksters together. I hope I was able to convey how all of their personalities go well together.

Book chat

Had you heard of any of the people, places or myths before reading this book?

Which tale or character did you like the best and why?

If you could ask any character from the book a question, who would you choose and why?

Who would you recommend this book to and why?

Do you have a favourite picture in the book?

Which of the tricksters do you think is the sneakiest? Why?

Which trickster would you like to learn more about?

If you had to think of a new title for the book, what would you choose?

Summarise this book in three sentences.

Book challenge:

Come up with your own trick to play and write down the steps.

Published by Collins An imprint of HarperCollins*Publishers*

The News Building
1 London Bridge Street
London
SE1 9GF
UK

Macken House
39/40 Mayor Street Upper
Dublin 1
D01 C9W8
Ireland

© HarperCollins*Publishers* Limited 2025

10 9 8 7 6 5 4 3 2 1

ISBN 978-0-00-874647-6

All rights reserved. No part of this publication may be reproduced, stored in a retrieval system, or transmitted in any form by any means, electronic, mechanical, photocopying, recording or otherwise, without the prior written permission of the Publisher or a licence permitting restricted copying in the United Kingdom issued by the Copyright Licensing Agency Ltd, 5th Floor, Shackleton House, 4 Battle Bridge Lane, London SE1 2HX.

Without limiting the author's and publisher's exclusive rights, any unauthorised use of this publication to train generative artificial intelligence (AI) technologies is expressly prohibited. HarperCollins also exercise their rights under Article 4(3) of the Digital Single Market Directive 2019/790 and expressly reserve this publication from the text and data mining exception.

British Library Cataloguing-in-Publication Data
A catalogue record for this publication is available from the British Library.

Download the teaching notes and word cards to accompany this book at:
http://littlewandle.org.uk/signupfluency/

Get the latest Collins Big Cat news at
collins.co.uk/collinsbigcat

Author: Jonny Walker
Illustrator: Corinne Caro (Astound Illustration)
Publisher: Laura White
Product managers: Caroline Green
and Holly Woolnough
Series editor: Charlotte Raby
Commissioning editor: Caroline Green
Development editor: Catherine Baker
Project manager: Emily Hooton
Copyeditor: Sally Byford
Proofreader: Catherine Dakin
Cover designer: Sarah Finan
Typesetter: 2Hoots Publishing Services Ltd
Production controller: Katharine Willard

Printed in the UK.

MIX
Paper | Supporting responsible forestry
FSC™ C007454

This book contains FSC™ certified paper and other controlled sources to ensure responsible forest management.
For more information visit: www.harpercollins.co.uk/green

Made with responsibly sourced paper and vegetable ink

Scan to see how we are reducing our environmental impact.

Acknowledgements
The publishers gratefully acknowledge the permission granted to reproduce the copyright material in this book. Every effort has been made to trace copyright holders and to obtain their permission for the use of copyright material. The publishers will gladly receive any information enabling them to rectify any error or omission at the first opportunity.

p27 Thomas Sanderhage/Shutterstock, p67t Imogen Warren/Shutterstock, p67b Peter J. Wilson/Shutterstock, p71 Martin and Carol/Shutterstock.